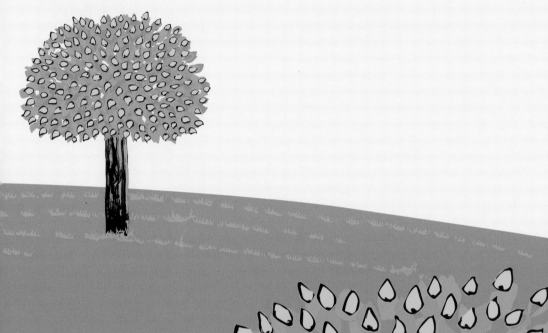

Jelleke Rijken and Mack van Gageldonk
Illustrated by Mack van Gageldonk

# Goodbye, Grandpa

Clavis

NEW YORK

It's early in the morning.

The sun has just come up, and Bear is waiting for Grandpa.

They're going fishing today. But where is Grandpa?

He should have been here by now.

Then Bear sees Bird flying toward him.

"Come!" Bird calls. "Come quick! Something's wrong."

Bear runs after Bird, as fast as he can.

*What's going on?* Bear thinks.

Then he sees Grandpa. But . . . why is Grandpa sleeping in the grass?

They were supposed to go fishing together, weren't they?

Bear tiptoes over to Grandpa.

"Grandpa, wake up!" Bear calls.

That's odd. Grandpa isn't waking up.

"Grandpa, wake up, please." Bear doesn't think it's funny.

He doesn't know what to do. Luckily Elephant is there.

Elephant carefully touches Grandpa's toes, Grandpa's heart,

and Grandpa's head with his trunk.

Then he makes a serious face.

"I know what's wrong with Grandpa . . ." he says.

"Grandpa has died."

Bear is so startled that he starts to cry. He cries so loud that Chicken hears him.

"Here I am," Chicken cackles. "Are you hurt?"

Bear takes a deep breath. "Grandpa is dead." Chicken doesn't understand.

Elephant tries to explain.

"When you're dead, you can't talk, move, or breathe.

You're no longer alive."

"How long does dead last?" Chicken wants to know.

"If you're dead, you can't be alive again. Ever!"

"My grandpa can!" Bear knows for sure.

"No, dear Bear, not even your grandpa," Elephant says softly.

"Bear, come here," Elephant whispers.

"We are going to say goodbye to your grandpa."

Bear wants to give Grandpa a gift.

He makes a drawing.

A drawing of a fish!

Chicken wants to do something too. She doesn't know what to make, but she has an idea. Grandpa loved yellow flowers. She is going to pick some!

Bear, Chicken and Elephant walk over to Grandpa
with the drawing and the flowers.
It feels weird, sad, and a little exciting, too.
No one knows what to say. So they don't say anything.

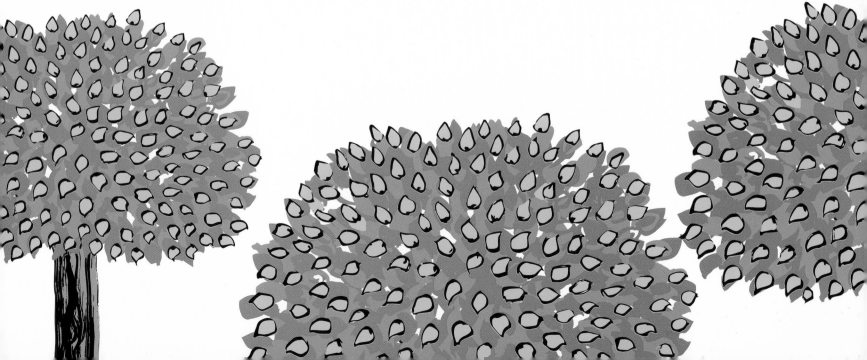

Grandpa is just lying there.
Leaves have fallen from the tree
and are covering him up.

Carefully, they approach Grandpa.

Chicken lays down her flowers and Elephant trumpets a song.

Then it's Bear's turn to say goodbye.
He finds a good spot for his drawing
and gives Grandpa one last long hug.

Bear and Elephant cover Grandpa with more leaves.

Chicken looks for branches.

She wants to build a campfire nearby.

They tell stories about Grandpa around the fire.
Grandpa could catch the biggest fish. He was not afraid to climb high up
in the trees. He was the sweetest grandpa you could ever imagine.
Suddenly Bear starts to cry really hard.
"Is Grandpa really gone for good? Will I never see him again?"

"Bear, close your eyes. What do you see now?" Chicken asks.

"Nothing."

"Look again, closely." Bear tries really hard, but nothing happens.

"Do you *hear* anything?" Elephant asks.

Bear cocks his fluffy ears.

"Can you still hear Grandpa's voice?"

Yes, Bear can hear it.

When he thinks of Grandpa, he hears him talking.

"And can you feel that Grandpa is close to you?"

Bear starts to cry again. He cries and cries and cries and cries.

Bear is sad, but he is happy, too.

Because now Bear understands.

All he has to do is close his eyes and Grandpa will be with him forever.

Night has fallen.

Bear, Elephant, and Chicken give each other one last hug.

It's time to go to bed. They'll see each other again in the morning.

"What shall we do tomorrow?"

"I know," Bear says. "Let's go fishing!"